Lulu is a star!

Praise for *Lulu and the Duck in the Park*

2013 ALSC Notable Children's Book

✩✩✩

2013 Book Links *Lasting Connection*

✩✩✩

2013 Booklist *Editors' Choice*

✩✩✩

2013 Chicago Public Library *Best of the Best*

✩✩✩

2012 Kirkus Reviews *Best Books of the Year*

✩✩✩

2013 USBBY *Outstanding International Book List*

✩✩✩

2013 CCBC Choice

✩✩✩

2013 ReadKiddoRead Kiddos Finalist

✩✩✩

A Junior Library Guild selection

✩

"McKay shows a rare ability to capture a younger audience in this involving chapter book for transitional readers. The well-structured, third-person narrative builds dramatic tension, provides comic relief of the most believable sort, and shows **plenty of heart**." —*Booklist* starred review

"A **warmhearted** beginning to a new chapter book series delights from the first few sentences...What Lulu and Mellie do to protect the egg, get through class, and not outrage Mrs. Holiday is told so simply and rhythmically and so true to the girls' perfectly-logical-for-third-graders' thinking, that **it will beguile young readers completely**."—*Kirkus Reviews* starred review

"McKay's pacing is **spot-on**, and the story moves briskly. Lamont's black-and-white illustrations capture the sparkle in Lulu's eyes and the warmth and fuzziness of a newly hatched duckling. The **satisfying** ending will have children awaiting the next installment in what is likely to become a hit series for fans of other plucky characters like Horrible Harry, Stink, and Junie B. Jones."—*School Library Journal* starred review

"'Lulu was famous for animals,' opens this **sparkling** series launch...This offering has...**abundant humor and heart**."—*Publishers Weekly* starred review

"McKay introduces complex characters, and animal-loving Lulu's dilemma **rings true**."—*Horn Book* starred review

Lulu
and the Duck in the Park

Hilary McKay
Illustrated by Priscilla Lamont

Albert Whitman & Company
Chicago, Illinois

Library of Congress Cataloging-in-Publication Data

McKay, Hilary.
Lulu and the duck in the park / by Hilary McKay ;
illustrated by Priscilla Lamont.
p. cm.—(Lulu ; 1)
Summary: Lulu, who loves animals, brings an abandoned
duck egg to school, even though her teacher has banned
Lulu from bringing animals to school ever again.
[1. Animals—Fiction. 2. Schools—Fiction. 3. Humorous stories.]
I. Lamont, Priscilla, ill. II. Title.
PZ7.M4786574Lu 2012
[Fic]—dc23
2012008229

Printed in the United States of America
10 9 8 7 6 5 4 3 2 LB 20 19 18 17 16 15

For more information about Albert Whitman & Company,
visit our web site at www.albertwhitman.com.

Chapter One
Lulu and Mellie

Lulu was famous for animals. Her famousness for animals was known throughout the whole neighborhood.

Animals mattered more to Lulu than anything else in the world. All animals, from the sponsored polar bear family that had been her best Christmas present, to the hairiest unwanted spider in the school coat room.

Lulu loved them all. She was always rescuing and comforting and carrying animals home.

Lulu might have been famous for other things, such as the way she ate apples, which left no apple at all, except the stalk and the seeds.

Or for jumping off swings, right at the highest point of the swing. (Swing jumping was a bad and dangerous habit of Lulu's that caused her many sore hands and scraped knees.)

"Crazy!" said Lulu's cousin Mellie when Lulu jumped off swings. It was usually

Mellie who hauled Lulu up after a swing jump and carried her bag while she hobbled home.

"Crazy! Nuts! Don't do it!" Mellie would say while Lulu inspected her new bruises, and she would nearly always add, "If you're going home now, can I come with you to see the animals?" Because whatever else Lulu did, it was her huge collection of animals that she was known for most of all.

"You know you can," Lulu would reply. "You always can. You know that."

Lulu and Mellie were best friends, as well as cousins. Mellie was famous for very long silences, sudden attacks of the giggles, and losing things. Hats and gloves, pencil cases and gym bags, school clothes and school books never seemed to stay

long with Mellie. They waited until she looked away, and vanished.

Mellie was very, very famous for losing things, but not as famous as Lulu was for animals.

It was lucky for Lulu that her father was famous for peering at the latest arrival and saying, "Hmmm. Well. Ask your mom."

And it was very lucky for Lulu that her mother was famous for saying, "The more, the merrier."

That was Lulu's mother's law on pets.

The More the Merrier,
As Long as Lulu Cleans Up after Them.

Lulu did not just clean up after them. She played with them and talked to them. She exercised them and fed them. She looked them up in library books and Googled them on the Internet. She thought about them.

"What would I want," wondered Lulu, "if I were a hamster in a cage? A spider in a bath? The Class Three guinea pig?"

Lulu's hamster had cardboard mazes to explore, and surprise parcels of nuts to unwrap. The spiders in Lulu's house had a little rope ladder to help them out of the bath. The Class Three guinea pig went home with Lulu for holidays and had a wonderful time going on outings to the park.

"Thank goodness I don't have to take him home," said Mrs. Holiday, Lulu's class teacher (famous for her cookie tin of exotic cookies and her icy-blue glares).

"*Mrs. Holiday!*" said Lulu, shocked. "He's an amazing guinea pig! For a guinea pig."

"I'm sure he is," agreed Mrs. Holiday. "But I am not a guinea pig sort of person. In fact," added Mrs. Holiday, "I could manage quite happily with no guinea pigs at all."

When the Class Three guinea pig was more annoying than usual (his bathroom habits were awful and he chewed up anything leaning against his cage), Mrs. Holiday would glare at him and say, "Hmmm!"

"Don't you like animals, Mrs. Holiday?" Lulu asked once.

"I like animals," said Mrs. Holiday, "in the wild. Perfectly happy, but a long way off!"

Lulu agreed about the animals being perfectly happy. That was good. But she did not agree about them being a long way off. *The closer the better*, Lulu thought.

"Perhaps you don't know many animals," she suggested to Mrs. Holiday.

"Hardly any," said Mrs. Holiday cheerfully.

Lulu tried to help with that.

She thought of lots of ways.

Mrs. Holiday would not be helped. She said, "No, no, no, absolutely not," when

Lulu offered to organize a pet show for the school summer fair.

"I'm not sure I want to look!" she said when Lulu brought in photographs of the Snail World she had built at the end of her garden. "Snails are just not me, Lulu! In fact, I'm afraid I don't like them much at all."

"It's not just snails," said Lulu. "Slugs too!"

"Even worse!" cried Mrs. Holiday.

Lulu bought a packet of dog treats, and a few days later her old dog, Sam, cleverly trailed her all the way to school.

Mrs. Holiday was not a bit pleased about that. Lulu was allowed to give him a drink of water, but after his drink Sam had to go to the janitor's room and be tied up until the end of the school day.

"Can't he stay with me?" begged Lulu.

"Certainly not," said Mrs. Holiday.

"He would be so good! You wouldn't even notice him!"

"I am noticing him already!" said Mrs. Holiday, glaring icy-blue glares at Sam, who was panting around the classroom, banging into things.

"He's a very nice dog," said Lulu pleadingly. "Look how friendly he is!"

Sam was now snuffling like a vacuum cleaner at the guinea pig cage. His snuffling made the guinea pig squeak and charge around, spilling wood shavings out through the bars.

"Woof!" said Sam loudly and happily.

"Lulu!" said Mrs. Holiday, handing Lulu a jump rope that she had cleverly knotted

to make a collar and leash. "Please take that very nice dog away *at once* and ask the janitor to keep him until it's time to go home."

"Now?" asked Lulu.

"This instant!" said Mrs. Holiday. "And while you are there, please borrow a dustpan and brush!"

So Lulu very slowly led Sam away, and when she came back the guinea pig was a lot calmer, and so was Mrs. Holiday. Until Lulu, busily sweeping, remarked, "I think the poor guinea pig needs a friend. I have some black-and-white mice. If you like I could bring them in to visit him. And I bet lots of the others have pets they could bring in too."

She was right. They did. They all offered at once to bring friends for the guinea pig. Class Three bounced in their seats in their eagerness to describe the friendliness of rats and lizards, cats and fish, turtles and tame(ish) beetles.

"No, no, no!" exclaimed Mrs. Holiday and called an emergency meeting for Class Three. And at the meeting she explained to everyone very carefully and plainly that if the Class Three guinea pig ever had a single friend brought in to visit…any sort of friend, a snaily friend or a whiskery friend, a very large friend like Sammy or a very small friend like a black-and-white mouse, then the Class Three guinea pig would unfortunately have to leave Class Three forever.

"But where would he go?" asked Lulu.

"*We would swap him for the Class Two stick insects!*" said Mrs. Holiday. "Class Two would be very pleased to swap," she continued, ignoring the howls and groans all around her, "and I would not mind a bit. I much prefer quiet unsmelly stick insects to squeaky rowdy guinea pigs. So. You have been warned!"

Class Three was silent with shock.

They all gazed at the guinea pig and thought how gloomy things would be without him. No more cheerful noisy

interruptions of squeaks in quiet lessons.
No more guinea-pig food to chew in
hungry moments. No more useful sausage-
shaped guinea-pig poops to flick around
the classroom.

At the end of the afternoon everyone
grumbled at Lulu for making Mrs. Holiday
think of such an awful idea.

They grumbled a lot, and the one who grumbled most of all was Mellie.

"Mrs. Holiday really meant it," said Mellie as she and Lulu swung in the little park together on their way home from school that day. "She would swap, I'm sure she would. And just looking at those stick insects makes me feel itchy all over. I think I may be allergic to them actually. So…"

There was a very long, swinging Mellie-style silence.

"I suppose I'd have to change schools," said Mellie.

"Oh," shouted Lulu. "Don't be silly!" And she swallowed the last of the apple she was eating, stuffed the stem and seeds in her pocket, jumped at the highest point of the swing, and after a wonderful, but

very brief, time flying through the air,
landed with a *smash*.

Then she gathered up Sam's jump rope
leash and hobbled away.

So Mellie, who was to have dinner with
Lulu that day, stopped her swing by scraping
her toes on the ground, and ran after her

(leaving her sweater hanging forgotten on the jungle gym).

They walked back to Lulu's house, arguing.

Lulu said it was not fair that the poor guinea pig had to live all alone with no friendly visitors.

Mellie said it was not fair if Lulu made Mrs. Holiday so angry that he had to be swapped for the Class Two stick insects.

Lulu made a list of all the quiet, peaceful animals she could bring to school that Mrs. Holiday would never notice. Mellie got angrier and angrier. The animals on the list got bigger and less quiet, just to annoy Mellie.

They did annoy Mellie.

"You just dare!" she said, when Lulu said rabbits in a backpack would never be noticed.

"Anyway, it would be cruel to the rabbits," said Mellie.

"Not at all," said Lulu. "They could wear sweaters and bounce around the play—"

"*Lulu!*" wailed Mellie.

"What?"

"Where's my sweater? My sweater's gone! Didn't I have it when I came out of school? Didn't I? I did! I know I did!"

"You must have left it by the swings," said Lulu, and they ran back together to see.

It was gone.

Mellie's things were always gone.

Mellie tipped her school bag upside down on the pavement to see if her sweater could possibly, magically, be at the bottom. Pencils and pens rolled everywhere and disappeared. A quarter spun neatly on its edge for a moment and vanished down a drain. Mellie sat down in the middle of the muddle and wailed, "It's all your fault, Lulu!"

She hated losing things.

Lulu collected books and pencils, hair clips, water bottles, homework sheets, and crumbled cookies. Sam licked Mellie's face, enjoying the taste of tears.

"I wouldn't have lost it if I hadn't been worrying about stick insects," said Mellie, sniffing and feeding Sam cookie crumbs while Lulu repacked her bag for her. "I just *don't* like stick insects!"

"Well, we won't have stick insects!" said Lulu kindly. "You can stop worrying. I won't bring visitors for the guinea pig, and Mrs. Holiday won't get mad and...*I know what will cheer you up!*"

Lulu scrambled out of her sweater, chewed off the name tag with her teeth, shook it out, and pulled it over Mellie's head.

"I've got another one at home," she said.

Chapter Two
Morning in the Park

Tuesday was Class Three's favorite day at school.

This was because Tuesday was swimming day.

The big swimming pool in the center of town was so close to school that Class Three did not have to take a bus to get there like other schools did. They could get there in a few minutes by walking.

First thing every Tuesday morning, Class Three walked down the hill from school, around the narrow cobbled streets by the church, and across the town park to the pool.

The town park was wonderful. Twenty times bigger than the little playing-field park where Mellie and Lulu swung after school.

It had huge trees and grassy slopes and twisting paths.

It had a climbing wall and a giant slide.

It had a candy shop and a life-size pirate ship becalmed in a sea of bark.

It had a lake with two little islands and a hundred noisy ducks.

Getting Class Three past the climbing wall without anyone climbing, and the candy shop without anyone darting in, and the lake without anyone getting wet, was the hardest part of Mrs. Holiday's week.

Getting them back to school again, wet-haired, starving, and weighed down by soggy swimming bags, was nearly impossible.

Mrs. Holiday didn't even try.

On Tuesday mornings after swimming, Mrs. Holiday marched Class Three to the bandstand by the lake. In the bandstand bags were dropped, boxes were opened, and Class Three ate their shivery bites.

That was what Mrs. Holiday, who had been brought up in Scotland, called the cookie-ish, appley, peanut-butter-sandwichy snack that came after swimming.

A shivery bite.

Mrs. Holiday was quite old. She had taught many, many classes of children. Some of them were grown up now, with families of their own. The things they had learned at school, the Romans and the Vikings, the way a bean grows in a jam jar, how to carry an egg on a spoon, and the names of the planets, had faded from their minds.

But none of them ever forgot their shivery bites.

After the shivery bites were eaten, Lulu and Mellie and the rest of Class Three were allowed ten minutes to climb aboard the pirate ship or slide down the giant slide or get stuck on the climbing wall.

Lulu always saved the end of her shivery bite for her favorite duck. It was a brown one, with one white wing.

The white-winged duck had a nest under the bushes on the bank by the path. It was so tame, it let Lulu come right up to visit.

"I would like to have a duck," Lulu often remarked.

For Class Three, that ten minutes in the town park was the best part of the whole cheerful morning. After it was over they went back to school and were good for a week so that they could do it all again after the next swimming lesson.

That was what usually happened on Tuesdays.

But this Tuesday was different.

This Tuesday—the day after Lulu's dog Sam trailed Lulu to school and Mellie lost her sweater and Class Three learned the very real danger of their guinea pig being swapped for a box of stick insects—the day after all that happened, things were very different and terrible in the park.

It was early spring. Every tree was exploding like a firework with bright green leaves. Every flower bed blazed with tulips and daffodils. And every one of the hundred ducks that lived by the lake had a nest of eggs or newly hatched ducklings. The white-winged duck was not the only one to make her nest among the bushes by the path. There was a whole line of them. "Duck Street," the park keepers called it.

There was a fine view of Duck Street from the bandstand.

Class Three had just unpacked their shivery bites when the trouble began. The park was suddenly filled with noise. Shouting and barking and running footsteps. The splashings and quackings of a hundred frightened ducks.

Two enormous dogs came tearing across the park toward Duck Street. Two big black dogs with thick leather collars. They were chasing the ducks and chasing each other and snarling and snapping. Flower beds were flattened. Ducks squawked in

panic and beat their wings. Ducklings fluttered and cheeped. And all along the Duck Street, under the new green bushes, nests were trodden on and scattered and smashed.

"NO!" screeched Lulu and ran to try and rescue her white-winged duck.

"No!" cried Mrs. Holiday and grabbed her just in time.

So Lulu had to watch.

For a long, long time no one could catch those terrible dogs. Not their owner with his two empty leashes, nor the park keepers who came running from every direction.

Those dogs were wild. And they ran so fast and they appeared so suddenly in so many unexpected places, that it seemed like there were far more than two.

"Keep those kids in the bandstand!" a

park keeper yelled at Mrs. Holiday, and she did. She stood at the top of the bandstand steps like a soldier on guard.

Class Three was screaming and pointing and shouting, and some of them were crying.

"Class Three, be silent, please!" commanded Mrs. Holiday.

Class Three became silent.

Then Mrs. Holiday took roll call, calling each person's name in turn, just like she did every morning at school. All through roll call she stood at the top of the steps, guarding the open entrance of the bandstand.

Now the bandstand was the quietest place in the park, but all around still the dogs ran wild.

One of them ran right up the bandstand steps.

"SIT!!!" bellowed Mrs. Holiday in a voice that no one in Class Three ever guessed she possessed.

A miracle happened.

Right in front of Mrs. Holiday, right under her icy-blue glare, the dog sat down.

His owner was there in a moment.

And two seconds later he was back on his leash.

The second dog did not even have to be told. He slunk toward the other dog with his tail between his legs.

Class Three yelled and cheered and clapped their heroic Mrs. Holiday, and as rapidly as they had arrived, the dogs vanished.

But the park was wrecked, and Duck Street was tragic.

Terrified ducks, huddled on the islands.

Lost ducklings.

Ruined nests.

Smashed and sticky eggs.

Class Three, walking two-by-two along the path by the lake, stepped carefully to avoid the scattered leaves and feathers of trodden nests. They tried not to look at the broken shells.

Lulu and Mellie were the last to leave the bandstand.

Mellie was still frightened. She looked anxiously behind them all the time, half expecting to see another huge dog exploding from the bushes.

She didn't see what Lulu saw.

There was not one unhurt nest left in Duck Street. The white-winged duck and her neighbors were all gone. But from the place where the white-winged duck had built her nest, something was rolling down the grassy bank.

A last blue egg from the Duck Street nests, the only one that hadn't been broken.

Faster and faster it rolled.

Any moment it would smash on the path.

Before Mellie turned around, before anyone saw, before she even thought what she was doing, Lulu had picked it up and put it in her pocket.

It was still warm.

Chapter Three
Life with an Egg

Lulu's hand curled around the egg in her fleecy jacket pocket, enjoying its polished roundness. It was not quite perfect, she discovered. There was a faint zigzag crack, so fine her fingers found it and lost it and found it again. There was a rough patch at one end where a fragment of shell was missing.

Well, thought Lulu, *it's had a terrible time, this egg! Of course there are bumps. A few bumps don't matter. Anyway, now it is safe.*

That was what Lulu thought. Nothing sensible, such as, *What am I going to do with this egg?* Or scary, such as, *What am I going to do with this egg if it breaks?*

She just plodded along beside Mellie and thought, *Safe.*

Mellie was also thinking. Not one thought, like Lulu. Lots of thoughts, barging into her brain from all directions.

I wish I had a tissue, Mellie thought. *A handkerchief. A paper towel. Something for my nose. It's the cold and the swimming-pool water making it run.*

Not crying.

Those dogs!

Those dogs should be arrested. Can you arrest dogs? Would they understand? They understood Mrs. Holiday when she said "Sit!"

Mrs. Holiday was…was…was…

Titanic! thought Mellie and skipped to have found the perfect word.

She skipped straight into the backs of Charlie and Henry, who were walking in front.

Henry (who always fell over at the smallest push) toppled right under her feet. Mellie tripped and fell on top of him, grabbing Lulu on the way down.

Lulu landed all curled up, wrapped around like a hedgehog with its paws in its pockets.

My egg! My egg! she thought, hardly daring to move for fear of what she might discover.

Mellie and Henry scrambled to their feet, blaming each other.

Charlie began a slow-motion action replay for anyone who had missed seeing the fun the first time around.

Mrs. Holiday came hurrying down the line of children, crying, "Everybody, quiet! Up you get, Lulu! Take my hand!"

Lulu, who was busy uncurling from around the egg, very slowly and carefully said, "No, no! Don't touch me! Leave me alone!"

"Are you hurt?" asked Mrs. Holiday, astonished at such rudeness.

Lulu didn't even hear her. Her fingers were exploring her pocket for damage. Was the egg broken? How broken? Fatally broken?

"Come on, Lulu!" said Mellie, tugging her arm impatiently. She looked shocked when Lulu pushed her away.

"Mellie was trying to help you!" snapped Mrs. Holiday, her eyes blue and icy.

Lulu, on her feet at last, gave a great sigh. Not broken. Wonderful.

"Sorry, Mellie," she said.

Mrs. Holiday was still angry.

"You can walk the rest of the way back to school with me!" she told Lulu. "Stand up properly, please, and take your hands out of your pockets…*Goodness, Charlie!*"

Charlie's nose was the sort that bleeds at the smallest excuse. Now a mixture of cold and swimming and excitement had started it again.

Blood was streaming down his face and splattering the pavement. Charlie, who always enjoyed the shrieks and fuss that went with nosebleeds, was bouncing with pleasure.

"I'm a vampire!" he called happily, diving for Henry's throat.

So in the end it was Charlie who had to walk with Mrs. Holiday with his swimming towel clutched to his nose, while Lulu and Mellie tagged along behind.

Every few minutes Mrs. Holiday glared over her shoulder at Lulu to make sure she knew she was still in trouble. Every few minutes Lulu looked unhappily down at the ground to show that she did.

Everyone was very relieved to get back to school.

Mrs. Holiday made a speech on the playground.

"It was a difficult morning for all of us," she said. "Difficult—Henry and Charlie, come and stand over here! Right beside me! One each side! How *very* silly!—Difficult and quite upsetting. I know we were all sad to see what happened in the park—Lulu, you look like you are trying to put your head in your pocket. It would be nice if you listened!—Now, Class Three! What have we learned to do at times like this? Do you remember? Yes, Mellie? Good girl!"

"Everyone should take handkerchiefs if they are going swimming," said Mellie.

"Because afterward the water runs out of your nose."

"Not quite what I was thinking of," said Mrs. Holiday, "but a sensible idea. I was hoping you would say we *learn*…What do we learn?"

"Shout 'Sit!' at mad dogs?" suggested someone.

"We *learn* that pets are a great responsibility," said Mrs. Holiday. "Isn't that true, Lulu?"

Lulu jumped guiltily.

"And when we have *learned*," continued Mrs. Holiday, "*we leave it behind* because… who wants to explain?"

"Because the ducks are all dead," said Henry.

"Because worrying does not change anything," said Mrs. Holiday. "(The ducks are not all dead. They may even lay eggs again.) We learn, leave it behind, and move on to make things better!"

That was what Mrs. Holiday always said after any awful event. The time the Class Three play for parents turned into a battle. The afternoon the Class Three soccer team lost ten–nothing to Class Two. The day the Lunch Lady Trick went wrong.

"How can we make this better?" inquired Mrs. Holiday now.

Class Three thought of lots of ways. Duck food to cheer up the ducks. A poster for the park saying PLEASE KEEP DOGS ON LEASHES. Zappers for park keepers so that

they could zap
mad dogs. Zappers
for ducks
so they could do
it themselves.

Lulu thought of
her egg and said
nothing.

"Lots of good
ideas!" said Mrs.
Holiday. "And
some not quite
so good. Charlie,
you will make
it start again,
doing that! There, now you've done it!
Come here! And the rest of you, jackets
off and reading books out while I look at
Charlie's nose."

Class Three streamed away to the coat

room. Lulu followed last of all. She had
forgotten she would have to take her jacket
off when she got back to school. *Thank
goodness for Charlie's nose*, she thought as
she waited for the others to leave the coat
room. It would keep Mrs. Holiday busy
for a few minutes while she, Lulu, took off
her jacket and found a safe place to keep a
large blue egg in a pocketless sweater.

Up the sleeves? Impossible.

Inside the front? Far too loose.

How on earth do ducks manage? wondered
Lulu, and she answered the question herself
a moment later: *nests*.

Lulu did not have a nest, but there were
plenty of woolly hats lying around by the
coat pegs. Lulu borrowed two and made a
hat nest, with one hat inside the other and
the egg warm in the middle.

The egg looked much safer in its hat nest.

Now what?
wondered Lulu.
*What do ducks do
with their nests?*

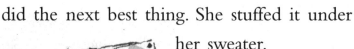

They sat on them.
Lulu could not sit
on her nest, but she
did the next best thing. She stuffed it under
her sweater.

Does it show?
wondered Lulu,
looking at her dim
reflection in the
mirror of the coat
room door.

It did, but not
terribly. And Mrs.
Holiday, Lulu was very
glad to see, was still
busy with Charlie.

So, feeling rather like a duck herself, Lulu waddled back to the classroom and sat down at the table she shared with Mellie.

Mellie had noticed.

"What have you got stuffed under your sweater?" she demanded.

"Under my sweater?"

"There's definitely something! Tell me! I won't tell."

"Well. A hat."

"A *hat*?"

"Yes."

"*Why?*"

"To keep it safe," replied Lulu, after some thought.

"Safe from what?"

"Getting lost."

"Oh," said Mellie in a rather surprised voice and then "Oh!" again in a rather impressed voice. *That isn't such a bad idea,* she thought. She might try it herself. Maybe she would not lose so many things, if she kept them stuffed safely under her sweater.

The only problem was:

"I lost my sweater," said Mellie, out loud. "This one I'm wearing is yours. Too tight for stuffing much under. OW!"

Mellie, experimenting with her pencil case, had stabbed herself with her ruler. That made Mrs. Holiday look over and say, "Mellie, please put your pencil case back on the table. It is time we all did some work. Everyone sit down! Charlie, hold that ice pack on your *nose*! It will never work there!"

"He doesn't want it to work," remarked Henry.

"Of course he does!" said Mrs. Holiday. "And anyway, all good things come to an end. Bloodletting is over. This is now math. Who can remember what we were talking about yesterday?"

Nobody could.

"Perimeters!" said Mrs. Holiday, writing the word on the board. "And where would we find a perimeter? You all knew yesterday!"

Class Three shook their heads. What they knew on one day had nothing to do with what they remembered the next.

"A perimeter," said Mrs. Holiday, "is a line that goes around the edge. A perimeter of a circle goes all around the edge of the circle. A perimeter of a field would go...Where would it go? Tell me, Henry!"

"In the grass," said Henry.

"All round the edge of the field," said Mrs. Holiday.

"That would be in the grass," said Henry. "Like I said."

"Today," continued Mrs. Holiday, ignoring Henry, "we are going to *measure* some perimeters! How could we measure a perimeter?"

"Is it a trick question?" inquired Mellie.

"No, it is a perfectly sensible question," said Mrs. Holiday patiently. "Lulu, why are you holding your stomach like that? Is everything all right?"

Lulu nodded and said, "Yes, thank you, Mrs. Holiday," although she was not quite certain that was true. A minute before, the hat nest had suddenly seemed to move. To shake, like a tummy rumble. Just for a moment. Perhaps it had been a tummy rumble.

"Good," said Mrs. Holiday, gathering up a pile of what looked like junk from the lost-and-found cupboard. "Now, we are going to investigate the perimeters of all these shapes. Working in pairs...There's a fan for you, Charlie and Henry! You girls can take these leaves. Who deserves the angel wings, I wonder?"

Up and down the classroom walked Mrs. Holiday, giving out strange objects to pairs of people. An enormous painted fan. A circle of curly cabbage leaves. A pair of cardboard angel's wings, a parasol, a pair of gloves, a T-shirt, and a kite.

"All these things have perimeters," she said. "This baby suit. This rather lovely peacock feather...You take that, Dan... On my table are pens and tape measures and all sizes of paper. First you must *estimate* (An estimate is a sensible guess, remember!) the perimeter of the object that I have given you, and then you must *measure* it...Think hard about how you will do that! Lulu and Mellie..."

She paused at their table. They were the last pair left without a shape to investigate, and her hands were empty.

"The perimeter of a person," she said. "Lulu, I think! Now then, Mellie! How will you investigate the perimeter of Lulu?"

"I know! I know!" said Mellie, rushing to the table to collect the largest piece of paper and the juiciest fat felt-tip

pen. "I know, I know, I know, don't
tell me!"

Mellie spread her piece of paper in the
middle of the classroom floor and pulled
the top off of her pen.

"Lie down, Lulu!" she ordered.

"*Mellie!*" moaned Lulu. "Lie down *there*?
Now?"

"Not now," said Mrs. Holiday, passing on
to another group of investigators. "First you
must estimate. Don't forget that!"

"First!" hissed Lulu. "You need to listen,
Mellie! I can't lie down there."

"You have to," said Mellie, testing her
green felt-tip pen on her arm. "Soon as
we've estimated. I estimate ten feet. Five up
one side and over your head. Five down the
other side and around your feet. Ten. Now
lie down!"

"Mellie, listen!" said Lulu. "Stop jumping

around and listen! It's not just a hat up my sweater. It's two hats…"

"Take 'em out!" said Mellie, waving her pen.

"And an egg."

"An *egg*?"

"A duck egg. From the park."

Mellie stared.

"It's still warm."

Mellie's eyes grew rounder and rounder.

"And I think…I think I felt it move!"

Mellie got the giggles of the most painful silent sort and lay on her stomach, weeping and gasping.

"It can't get broken," hissed Lulu, shaking her, "because then there would be a duckling. A duckling!"

Here in this classroom! And you know
what Mrs. Holiday said yesterday about
no more animals!"

"Oh," said Mellie, suddenly becoming
calm. "Not good."

She looked across the room at the guinea
pig who might so easily be swapped for
stick insects.

And then
Mellie became
wonderful.

In no time the piece of paper for Lulu to lie on was whisked to the Reading Corner, the most private place in the classroom. Then, in one green juicy line, Mellie drew all around the edge of her friend. Before anyone had noticed anything unusual about Lulu's sweater at all, they were back at the table again and marking off the perimeter of a person in neat green inches.

"Exactly what I hoped you would do," said Mrs. Holiday when she came to see how they were getting on.

"Eggsactly!" whispered Mellie when she had gone and gave one of her sudden snorts of laughter. "Is it still safe?"

"I think so. I hope so. If I can just keep it not broken until after school. Then I'm going to ask Mom to let me take it to the vet."

"Yes, he'll know how to hatch it," agreed
Mellie. "And then you'll have a duckling.
Lucky thing!"

"I'll share."

"It will need a pond."

"How hard is it to dig a pond?" asked
Lulu.

"I'll help," said Mellie.

Lulu became much happier. Life with a
hat nest under her sweater was much easier
with a friend who understood.

Mellie was very useful. When Lulu
needed to fetch or pick up or hold, Mellie
was there to help. At lunchtime she was
a human shield that stopped the hat nest
from being squashed in the lunchtime line.
After lunch, when the rest of the school
was charging around the playground,
she visited the library and found a book
on ducks.

The book made Lulu and Mellie rather sad.
Mother ducks, it said, talked to their
ducklings before they were even hatched.

"They talk to their *eggs*?" asked Mellie,
astonished.

"And the ducklings inside the eggs learn
the sound of their mothers' voices," read

Lulu. "And the ducklings talk back to their mothers! Oh my poor white-winged duck!"

"I don't think that can be true," said Mellie. "I don't see how anything could make a sound in an egg!"

"Just in case," said Lulu, worrying, "I should quack to this egg. So it doesn't get lonely."

"Should I quack too?" asked Mellie. "Would it help?"

Lulu said she thought that would help a lot, and it did. She felt much less silly quacking with a friend than quacking alone.

After lunch came music. That was difficult. Class Three was practicing a song for the Easter play, with singers and recorders. Mellie's recorder had been lost months before, but Lulu still had hers. There was no possible excuse that could save her from having to stand in front of the class

with the rest of the recorder group and play
her recorder.

"I'll take care of the egg," said Mellie
bravely, and she did. For the next half hour
she cradled the hat nest in her hands under
the table, hardly daring to breathe.

Music passed safely.

The day that had begun in such a fuss
of water and dogs and quacking and tears
became more and more peaceful. Mrs.
Holiday handed out doodling paper and
picked up a new storybook.

"*Harry Potter*," she read, "*and the Sorcerer's Stone.*"

She had been promising to begin it for weeks.

CRACK!

Even through two hats and her sweater, Lulu felt that crack.

Chapter Four
Life with a Duck

Lulu looked across at Mellie to see if she had noticed anything. Mellie was in a Mellie-dream, tilting her chair backward, listening to the story while she drew owls and ducks and lightning-shaped scars.

Maybe I imagined it, thought Lulu, and she began very carefully to move her hand under her sweater, over the rim of the hat nest, down toward the egg.

Something?

Nothing?

Lulu jumped with shock.

No more smooth egg.
Fragments of shell.
No more
warm stillness. A
fluttering struggle
for freedom.
No more
quiet. A thin,
high voice.
"Weep!"
wheezed the

front of Lulu's sweater. "Weep!"

"Is someone trying to be funny?"
demanded Mrs. Holiday, looking up from
her book.

Luckily for Lulu, several people were
goofing off. Charlie and Henry were
thumb wrestling. Someone else was
having a tug of war with the guinea pig

over a spelling list. Mellie fell off her chair.

Mrs. Holiday snapped *Harry Potter* shut.

"Oh, Mrs. Holiday!" groaned Class Three.

"*If* you would like me to read any more," said Mrs. Holiday, glaring, "you will become instantly quiet and sensible. *If* you would not like me to read any more, then we will spend the time on mental math!"

Class Three became instantly quiet and sensible. Mrs. Holiday began reading once more. Lulu wrote *It's hatching* on her doodling paper, nudged Mellie, and pointed.

Mellie stared.

Now? she wrote.

Lulu nodded.

Did you bump it?

"No," whispered Lulu.

On its own?

"Yes."

"I didn't know they did that," whispered Mellie. "Not on their own! From the inside. I thought the mother duck helped them break their way out."

"Mellie!" exclaimed Mrs. Holiday. "Collect your things together and come and sit by me!"

Mellie did. But not before she had scrawled on her doodling paper: *Wontitsuffket* and pushed the paper toward Lulu.

Wontitsuffket, read Lulu, puzzled. *Wontitsuffket? What is* wontitsuffket?

She looked at Mellie.

Mellie looked desperately back.

Won, read Lulu again. *Or Wont? Wont it? Wont it suffket.*

OH!

Won't it suffocate?

"Please, Mrs. Holiday," begged Lulu, "may I leave the room? Now? Quick?"

Mrs. Holiday nodded and then noticed Lulu's hands holding the front of her sweater and said, "Yes, you may. Now! Quickly! Mellie, go with her. Come back for me if Lulu is not well."

"Hurry!" added Mrs. Holiday urgently, because if there was one thing she could not bear, it was people being ill in her classroom.

Lulu and Mellie hurried. They raced along the corridor, burst into the empty bathroom, thankfully shut the door, and leaned on it.

"Get it out! Get it out!" begged Mellie.

Lulu was already doing that. Her sweater was off. The hat nest was in her hand. She was turning back the rim.

"Weep!" called the occupant suddenly. "Weep! Weep! Weep!"

There it was: a duckling. A fluffy head, already dry. Two questioning, shining black

eyes. Two stumpy wings, fluttering in
the sudden light. The rest still hidden in
the shell.

"Weep!" called the duckling, a dry, thirsty
call.

"It really is!" said Mellie. "It really, really
is a real actual duckling!"

"Weep," insisted the duckling.

"What does it want?"

"Could it want a drink?" wondered Lulu. She wet her finger and held it so that a drop of warm water touched the duckling's beak.

"Weep!" it said and swallowed the drop and then another and another, and then it fluttered with sudden energy and stepped out of its shell.

Lulu and Mellie forgot the classroom. They forgot Mrs. Holiday and *Harry Potter*. They forgot the guinea pig and the park. They sat on the cold bathroom floor with the hat nest between them, and for a long time all they said was: "Look!" and "Oh!" and "Did you see that?"

In the classroom Mrs. Holiday was having a hard time. Class Three said she was not reading *Harry Potter* properly. They knew this was true because they had all seen the

movie. They kept putting up their hands to
complain, saying things like:

"Are you skipping bits, Mrs. Holiday?"
and, "She's not skipping bits, she's putting
extra bits in," and, "When will we get to
the train?" and, "My mom read it to me
and there was nothing about drills," and,
"Hagrid didn't talk like that!"

It seemed to poor Mrs. Holiday that every time she looked up, dozens of hands were waving in the air. Each hand was attached to a complaining listener.

"If you would like me to read you a book that has not been made into a movie, I can do that very easily," said Mrs. Holiday at last and picked up *Key Stage 2 Mental Math*.

The waving hands vanished and Harry Potter's adventures continued. But after a while the questions began again.

"Is this book true?" and, "Mrs. Holiday, can you do magic?" and, "I've never seen an owl."

"*I've* never seen a rat."

"I've never seen a *toad*."

"I've never seen an owl or a rat or a toad!"

"Hands down!" roared Mrs. Holiday,

unable to bear one second more. "Yes, you too, Henry! Whatever it is, I don't want to know!"

So Henry sat quietly and did not tell her that the guinea pig was out until it actually vanished along the windowsill and out of the window.

That was why it wasn't for a while, not until the guinea pig was tracked down and recaptured and the window closed

and everyone sitting quietly on their hands doing mental math, that Mrs. Holiday remembered Lulu and Mellie.

"We have to go back to class," Mellie was saying to Lulu. "I have to anyway, otherwise Mrs. Holiday will think you are sick. I'm surprised she hasn't remem—"

That was when Mrs. Holiday charged into the bathroom.

Chapter Five
Afternoon in the Park

Mrs. Holiday stood in the bathroom doorway and looked down at Lulu and Mellie and the duckling, all together on the bathroom floor, and her mouth opened and closed and opened and closed like a duck that had lost its quack.

"Lulu!" she said at last.

"Mrs. Holiday," said Lulu earnestly. "I didn't bring this duckling to school. I didn't bring any animal to school. I promise I didn't."

"Please don't swap the guinea pig for those awful stick insects," pleaded Mellie.

"It was only an egg when I picked it up," explained Lulu. "You can't call an egg an animal."

"Lots of people bring eggs to school," pointed out Mellie. "Packed lunches."

"Weep!" said the duckling.

"It rolled out from the bush where the white-winged duck had her nest," said Lulu. "I picked it up just before it got smashed

on the path. All the other eggs were broken. I was going to take it to the vet."

"Oh, Lulu," said Mrs. Holiday, sighing.

"She made it a hat nest to keep it safe," said Mellie. "But it hatched anyway."

"*Where* did it hatch?" asked Mrs. Holiday.

"Under my sweater," said Lulu.

"Lulu," said Mrs. Holiday, "I have been teaching in schools for twenty-seven years. In all those twenty-seven years, no one has ever hatched a duckling under their sweater..."

Mrs. Holiday paused to take a very clean folded handkerchief out from her pocket. She dabbed it carefully at the corner of each of her eyes.

"...as far as I know," said Mrs. Holiday and dabbed her eyes again.

Was she laughing or was she crying? Lulu and Mellie could not tell.

"Well," said Mrs. Holiday, putting her handkerchief away and becoming her old bossy self again. "This is no place for a duckling. It belongs in the park. Maybe… maybe…You girls wait here!"

With that she was gone, and Lulu and Mellie were left staring at each other.

"Was she angry?" wondered Lulu, but Mellie shook her head and said she did not know.

The duckling was crying again. "Weep, weep." A lost, unhappy sound.

Lulu looked around the room. She saw bright, shabby paint and the underside of sinks. Drain pipes and tiles. A notice on the door: DON'T FORGET TO WASH YOUR HANDS!

Mrs. Holiday is right, Lulu thought. *This is no place for a duckling.*

She was still thinking this when Mrs. Holiday came back. She was carrying a box

and she was in a great rush.

"We have twenty-five minutes until the bell rings," she told Lulu and Mellie. "Hurry up! The secretary has very kindly agreed to stay with Class Three (heaven help her). Get your jackets, girls, and we will go back to the park. Perhaps we can find the duck with the white wing and give her back her duckling again."

In no time the duckling was rushed into the box.

The secretary was given Mrs. Holiday's exotic cookie tin to use as a last resort.

And then Lulu and Mellie and Mrs. Holiday set off to find the duck with the white wing, in spring sunshine that felt as warm as summer.

The park was as quiet as if nothing had happened. The paths were swept clean of spoiled nests and broken shells. The flower beds were tidy again. No huge silly dogs tore through the bushes. No children squealed in the bandstand. On the lake the ducks were almost silent. Some of them slept on the little islands, one eye open, one leg tucked up. Little chains of ducklings looped in and out of the reeds at the edge.

"Measuring the perimeter," said Mellie.

But on the bank by the bandstand a brown duck with a white wing searched among the bushes. Searched and searched and called and called.

"Weep! Weep!" cried the duckling from the box in Lulu's hand.

The duck
with the
white wing
paused.

"She's
listening,"

whispered Mellie. "Hurry, Lulu!"

So Lulu lifted the duckling from the hat nest and tucked him back under the

bushes where he had lived so long as
an egg.

He was hardly alone for a moment.

Lulu and Mellie and Mrs. Holiday sighed
great sighs of happiness and relief and went
back to school just in time for the bell to
go home.

"What a day!" groaned Mrs. Holiday,
collapsing like a rag doll in a staff room
chair. "What a day, what a day!"

Lulu and Mellie walked home together with
Charlie and Henry.

They stopped to swing in the little park,
all four in a row, which took up all the
swings.

"You missed tons when you disappeared
this afternoon," Charlie told Lulu and
Mellie as they swung. "Mrs. Holiday trying

to read *Harry Potter* and then going crazy. Mental math when nobody knew a single answer. The guinea pig escaping out of the window. The secretary and the cookie tin. We ate every single cookie in Mrs. Holiday's special tin! The secretary made us do who-can-hold-their-breath-the-longest competitions and gave them out as prizes."

"You missed the park, though," said Mellie cheerfully, swinging so high and so wildly that hair clips tumbled from her hair and were lost in the grass forever.

"We didn't. Not really. We were there this morning."

"This morning," said Mellie, "was completely different from this afternoon."

This morning, remembered Lulu, *I found my egg. I miss my egg.*

"Better or worse?" demanded Henry.

"Which was this afternoon? Better or worse?"

Although, thought Lulu, *there are things you can't do with an egg up your sweater.*

"Better or worse?" echoed Charlie.

Lulu waited until her swing reached its farthest point forward, let go, and flew.

"A million times better!" she shouted and landed in a heap.

"Crazy!" said Mellie, scuffing with her toes to make her own swing stop. "Crazy! Nuts! You just shouldn't do it, Lulu!"

"You say that every time!"

"If you're going home now, can I come with you to see the animals?"

"You know you can."

"Can we come too?" asked Charlie.

Lulu nodded.

"The rabbits and the parrot? Snail World and Sam? The hamster and those black-and-white mice? All of them?"

"All of them, except my duckling," said Lulu. "I keep him in the park!"

Turn the page for a
sneak peek at the next

Lulu

adventure!

When Lulu goes on vacation, she finds a
dog living on the beach. Everyone in the
town thinks the dog is trouble. But Lulu is
sure he just needs a friend. And that he's
been waiting for someone just like her...

Chapter One

The Cottage by the Sea

Lulu and Mellie were seven years old. They
were cousins and they
were friends. Their
houses were so close
that it took less than
five minutes to run
between the two. They
could visit each other
easily without getting
lost or squished on
the road.

That was a good thing, because Lulu and Mellie were not just ordinary friends—they were best friends.

They were such good friends they hardly ever fought, although sometimes they did grumble at each other a little. They mostly grumbled about each other's hobbies, which were not at all alike.

"Coloring again?" Lulu would say when she went to see why Mellie had forgotten to come and play. "You're *always* coloring!"

"Cleaning again?" Mellie would ask when she came to find out what Lulu had been doing all day. "You're *always* cleaning!" she would say, holding her nose.

It wasn't true that Mellie was always coloring. Often she was painting or drawing or making things with glue and glitter and chopped-up paper and causing

a mess. But it was true that very often Lulu
was cleaning.

Lulu loved animals and she had a lot
of pets.

The rule about pets in Lulu's house was:
*The more the merrier! As long as Lulu cleans
up after them!*

Lulu had two guinea pigs, four rabbits,
one parrot, one hamster, a lot of goldfish,
and a rather old dog named Sam.

It took a lot of work to look after all these pets. Mostly Lulu did it, but sometimes other people helped her out.

Whenever Lulu's family went on vacation, Mellie's parents would always help. They would do a swap—Lulu's family would take Mellie on vacation, and Mellie's family would take care of Lulu's pets.

All except for Sam the dog, who was going on vacation too. They were all going to stay in a cottage by the sea.

Sam did not think much of that. He didn't enjoy the seaside. He wasn't fond of sand, he didn't like chilly breezes, and he hated getting wet in cold, salty water. Sam was a small, golden, teddy-bear-shaped dog. He had short teddy bear legs, and a round teddy bear tummy, and a sweet, stubborn, sleepy teddy bear face.

When Sam went on vacation he took a

lot of luggage, all packed for him by Lulu.
He took his red blanket and his water
bowl and his food dish and his special dog
biscuits. Also his dog leash and his dog
towels in case he got wet, and his shampoo
and his brushes in case he got sticky.

Sam also took his basket and his red
velvety beanbag.

Sam loved his beanbag very much and if

he did not have it in his basket he could not go to sleep. Nobody else could go to sleep either, because Sam walked around howling and whining and moaning. It was very important not to forget the beanbag. Lulu's father checked a dozen times that it was safely in the car. He did not want to have to drive all the way home for it in the middle of the night, as he had once had to do.

Sam's luggage took up so much space that it was a good thing Lulu and Mellie had brought as little as possible. Their only big thing was Mellie's build-your-own-kite-kit. Mellie had been given this for a birthday present. She had opened it to admire the strings and the special kite paper, the bright pens, and the exciting instructions. But then she had put it away again to save for this seaside vacation.

Now the kite kit was on the backseat. All the things that would not fit anywhere else were there too, piled around Lulu and Mellie.

"It's part of the vacation feeling," said Mellie. "Being all squished up, hardly able to breathe."

"It's fair that Sam should have the most space," agreed Lulu, "because really he'd rather not come on vacation at all. He'd rather be comfortable."

"This might be a comfortable vacation!" said Lulu's mother hopefully. That made everyone hoot with laughter. They spent the first part of the journey reminding one another about vacations in the past.

"Like the time we went camping and left behind the bag that had everyone's shoes," said Lulu.

"Or that house we stayed in that had a ghost in the attic," said Mellie.

"Or that place where the chimney was struck by lightning and fell down into the living room," said Lulu's father.

Lulu's mother groaned and said perhaps they should turn back and not go away after all.

"They were nice vacations," said Lulu and Mellie, who had enjoyed the lightning and the ghost and the new shoes very much.

They were really looking forward to staying in a little seaside town.

That was what they thought, but the first thing they discovered about the cottage was that it was not near the town at all. It was all on its own, down a bumpy, potholed road. Bumps made Sam sick. So Lulu's father drove very slowly, trying to dodge the biggest holes, while Lulu's mother twisted around, watching for the gulps that meant Sam had to be flung out of the car as quickly as possible. Meanwhile, Mellie was ignoring both Sam and the bumpy road and saying, "Should I unpack my kite now, now that we're almost there? I think I could just open it and get out the parts…"

"No!" said Lulu's mother and father, but they said it too late. Mellie was already unpacking the kit. When the car fell into another hole, important-looking pieces of kite spilled everywhere, and Mellie began to moan.

"Just what I didn't want to happen!" she grumbled, turning herself upside down to try and gather the pieces from the floor.

"They call this a road?" complained Lulu's father. "It's just one giant crater after another!"

"Now the string's unwound!" cried Mellie.

Sam made a noise like a sort of cough.

"Almost there, Sam!" said Lulu's mother hopefully, rolling down her window.

Only Lulu sat quietly, gazing at the view. Ahead, she saw a white cottage and green grass. Every few minutes, she saw glimpses of a sea that gleamed dark gray or silver bright.

All along the edge of the sea Lulu could see a mountain range of sand dunes. Strange bushes grew on them with

dim gray leaves and orange berries.
Strange ribbonlike blue-green grasses were
combed by the sea wind. Strange narrow
sandy paths twisted and climbed and
suddenly vanished.

And all among the bushes and grass and
sandy paths a strange animal leaped and ran,
watching the car. It moved so quickly that
the only thing Lulu could see clearly was
its strange, flapping ears.

They were ears like brown paper bags.

The owner of the cottage was waiting for them when they arrived. Everyone except Mellie (who was still picking up pieces of kite) tumbled out of the car, all stiff and achy from traveling.

"Took your time, didn't you?" said the cottage owner as Lulu's parents smiled and called hello. "I saw you, dithering along that road, like there was all the time in the world!"

"Well!" began Lulu's father. "It's quite an obstacle course, that road..."

"You've got the wrong kind of car!" said the cottage owner. "You need something much bigger! Hurry up! Come inside and I'll give you the key. Shoes off!" she added sternly.

"It's very kind of you to wait," said Lulu's

mother, as she and Lulu's
father followed her to
the door.

"Had to," snapped the
cottage owner grimly.
"I needed to warn you
about that dog!"

"Sam?" asked Lulu, but
the cottage owner had
disappeared, with Lulu's
parents after her.

Bang! went the door in a
most unfriendly way.

"Why's she so…"
began Mellie, staring.

"Shush!" warned Lulu.

"…angry?" finished Mellie loudly, dropping
pieces of kite all over the ground as she spoke.
"Don't worry! She can't hear! She shut the door.
Why do you think she said that about Sam?"

Lulu couldn't imagine. Sam was behaving perfectly. He had survived the bumps without getting sick, and now he was doing what he always did at the end of a car journey: unpacking his food bowl.

On days when Sam was going for a ride in the car he was only ever given a very small breakfast. Now he wanted the rest of it. He stood up on his teddy bear legs, dragged his bowl out from his mountain of luggage, carried it in his teeth to Lulu, and dropped it at her feet.

It was Lulu's job to fill it up as quickly as possible.

As usual, she rushed to do it, and as usual Sam stood and watched, stumpy tail wagging, with a smile on his teddy bear face.

From inside the cottage Lulu's parents could see all this happening. Lulu's mother asked worriedly, "Why do you want to warn us about our dog? We did tell you we were bringing him."

"Your dog?" asked the cottage owner, looking out of the window at the happy sight of Sam gobbling dog food. "I wasn't talking about your dog! He's a poor old thing, isn't he? Looks more like a sheep... *That* dog!"

She jabbed a pointing finger in the direction of the sand dunes, where a small sandstorm had just erupted.

The sandstorm rolled down the sand dunes, arrived between Lulu and Mellie in a cloud of dust, seized the packet of dog food that Lulu had only a moment before put down, whirled around, and raced away, all in one astonishing moment.

"*RUFF! RUFF! RUFF!*" barked Sam, nearly falling over with rage.

"*That* dog!" said the cottage owner, rushing out of the cottage with Lulu's parents behind her. "That dog!" she repeated, pointing to a dusty blur on the sand dunes. "That dog from the sea! He's a thief! He's a menace! The people last week lost a whole roasted chicken from under their noses! Nothing is safe from him and no one can get near him. We've had the dogcatcher out twice already and he's never gotten close enough to grab—"

"Oh, poor dog!" exclaimed Lulu.

"Don't you go encouraging him," said the woman, turning on Lulu quite fiercely. "He's not welcome around here! You'll have to be careful. No leaving out picnics or scraps for the seagulls. He goes through all the trash too. So you'll have to remember to take the trash can into the house at night!"

"*Take the trash can into the house at night?*" repeated Lulu's father, staring.

"I've warned you and now I need to go," said the cottage owner.

"Did you say, 'Take…'?"

"I did," said the cottage owner, dragging a bike from the hedge. Then she handed Lulu's mother a large and rather rusty key and rode off.

"*Take the trash can into the house at night!*" exploded Lulu's father wildly the moment she was gone. "What kind of place is it where you have to do that?"

Lulu and Mellie became helpless with giggles and rolled around on the grass.

"And you're not helping!" complained Lulu's father as he stepped over them.

"Oh!" said Mellie. "I love this place!"